Way Up and Over Everything

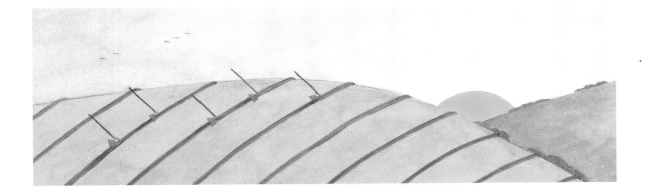

This book is dedicated to my sisters Dewildera and Mayner and to my grandson, Darryl. They remember our stories. —A.M.

For Magriet, with love. —J.D.

Text copyright © 2008 by Alice McGill
Illustrations copyright © 2008 by Jude Daly

www.houghtonmifflinbooks.com

The text of this book is set in Calisto.
The illustrations are watercolor.

Library of Congress Cataloging-in-Publication Data
McGill, Alice.
  Way up and over everything / Alice McGill.
       p. cm.
Summary: In this retelling of a folktale, five Africans escape the horrors of slavery by simply disappearing into thin air.
  ISBN 0-618-38796-X
 [1. Folklore—United States. 2. African Americans—Folklore. 3. Slavery—Folklore.] I. Title.
PZ8.1.M1713Way 2005
398.2—dc22   2003019384

ISBN-13: 978-0-618-38796-0

Printed in Singapore

TWP 10 9 8 7 6 5 4 3 2 1

Way Up and Over Everything

Alice McGill

Illustrated by Jude Daly

HOUGHTON MIFFLIN COMPANY
BOSTON 2008

My great-grandmama's mama told her and she told me this story about a long time ago.

My great-grandmama's mama was named Jane. She was born and raised near the coast of Georgia on the plantation of Ol' Man Deboreaux; that's what the enslaved people called him behind his back. To his face, they called him "master."

Jane was around sixteen years old in 1842. That spring, she said, word spread among the enslaved that Ol' Man Deboreaux had bought five new Africans off the boat in Charleston. From there, he sent

them to a place behind Deep Woods to teach them how to work in the fields and how to talk just like I'm talking to you right now.

Anyhow, one morning at daybreak, just at eating time, the overseer led a mule and wagon into the quarters.

There on the wagon bed sat two young men and three young women—chained together. The quarters' up-in-age women, Sis Bellah and Sis Sarah, ceased stirring the cooking pots. A crowd of grown folks and children standing in the eating line stared at them.

The two young men in the
wagon kept looking round at
the cabins, peach trees, and up
toward Ol' Man Deboreaux's
house.

Calm-like, the African
women turned their smooth dark
faces to watch the overseer
unlock the last set of chains.

"Get off this wagon!" the overseer shouted. The new Africans scooted off and onto the ground.

Ol' Man Deboreaux walked up. "They work in the fields today," he told the overseer.

"Mister Deboreaux, sir," the overseer said, "I thought you said for me to train them more first."

"They work today," Ol' Man Deboreaux said. With that, he went stepping back to his big house.

The overseer pointed to the eating line and shouted, "Get over there!"

Sis Sarah quickly called out to everybody. "Y'all move back. Let the new folks get eats first—like company."

Before Jane could move aside, one of the young men stepped in line behind her. She turned to get a good look at him. Quietly, he smiled at her, touched his chest, and whispered, "Edet, Edet," like he was telling her his name.

"Shut your mouth, Bob!" the overseer shouted. "You know what your name is now!"

The one called Bob closed his mouth.

After Sis Sarah scooped boiled beans and ham skins into tin bowls for them, they all sat on wooden benches and got done eating right quick and quiet.

Before long, the overseer returned on horseback. Folks ran to grab hoes, then followed the overseer on foot. Fields of cotton had to be planted. The new Africans would have to learn hard work by the whip for the

rest of their lives. If a hoe rested too long, the whip popped. If cottonseeds didn't hit the dirt fast enough, the whip popped. Nobody could tell from what direction the sound of the whip would pop.

Just before sundown, the up-in-age women clapped the eating-time bell. The overseer rode on up toward the big house. Hungry and thirsty, the slaves gathered round cool buckets of water and the cooking pot. But the new Africans waited on the side like thirst and hunger didn't bother them at all.

When the crowd thinned out, Jane noticed that the Africans no longer waited on the side. They were gone! Folks searched the cabins, the barns, and the grape arbor. The Africans could not be found.

When somebody raced up to the big house and told Ol' Man Deboreaux, he ran out, hollering, "Get the dogs! Hurrup, get the dogs!"

Folks hid in the cabins when the overseer put the leashes on them growling, trying-to-get-away dogs.

Jane didn't hide. She was scared, though. The dogs, picking up the scent from where the Africans had sat in the wagon, pulled the overseer back to the field. Ol' Man Deboreaux lagged behind the overseer, puffing and sweating.

Jane crept along the outer edge of the field, hoping she could somehow warn the new Africans. She trailed Ol' Man Deboreaux to the rise in the middle of the field. There, in a circle some distance away, the five Africans stood holding hands—and looking up at the sky. *"Ndiseh Fe! Ndiseh Fe!"* they called out in their own African speech.

The overseer ran faster. "I got you now!" he shouted.

But the Africans started whirling round in the circle so fast that their feet looked apart from their legs.

By the time Jane and Ol' Man Deboreaux reached them, one African woman dropped hands and stepped up on the air—like she was climbing a ladder. Then she moved her arms like wings and her feet like tail feathers, and she flew! And before she could get out of sight, another stepped up on the air, and then another.

The dogs snarled. Ol' Man Deboreaux rubbed his face like his eyes didn't know how to tell him the truth. "Stop that!" he ordered. "I paid for you—you belong to me."

The Africans kept climbing up on the air until only one was left—the one who had smiled at my great-grandmama's mama, Jane. Well, seem like he just took his own lonesome time and hovered there in the air.

"Catch him!" Ol' Man Deboreaux cried.

The overseer jumped up and almost grabbed his foot. But the one they called Bob, he just stepped higher and higher.

Then he turned to look down at my great-grandmama's mama and touched his chest. His loud voice filled the air with "Edet! Edet!"— like he was telling the whole wide world his real name.

"Edet! E-det!" Jane shouted up to him. "Take me with you!" But Edet kept treading air with arms like wings. His feet moved like tail feathers and he sailed beyond the clouds, way up and over everything.

Had they gone back home to Africa? Jane wondered as she waved goodbye. She hoped so.

Ol' Man Deboreaux stared and stared at the sky like the Africans would come back. Finally, he said to the overseer, "If I hear any talk of this, you will lose your position. And you, gal— which one are you?"

"Jane," my great-grandmama's mama said loud and clear.

"Well, Jane, if you tell one word about this to anyone, I will sell you down the river!"

But Jane did tell. She told this story when she was a slave living in the quarters and she told it after she and her children escaped to freedom.

And her children told this story too.

You see, my great-grandmama's mama told her and she told me about this story about a long time ago when Africans could fly just like birds—

way up and over everything.

ABOUT THIS STORY

The gift of flying was created by a wish for freedom. The first African slaves were captured from their villages and shipped to America about four hundred years ago. Many of those people suffered and died during the long journey known as the Middle Passage. Those who survived landed at waterfronts to be sold to the highest bidder. For the rest of their lives, Africans were forced to work without pay for slaveholders.

The Africans had to leave their language behind. Therefore, they learned to speak American English in many

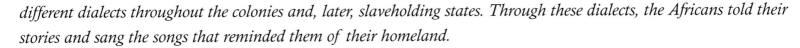

different dialects throughout the colonies and, later, slaveholding states. Through these dialects, the Africans told their stories and sang the songs that reminded them of their homeland.

According to the traditional stories, people trying to escape mysteriously disappeared into thin air. Those left behind sang songs and told stories about these flying folks. Sometimes, the stories said, a hoe continued to work in the field after the Africans had flown away.

People of African descent continued to tell the "flying stories" many generations after the Civil War ended in 1865.

Now I tell the flying story that was passed down in my family through Mama Jane, born in 1857. She was named after her mother, the Jane in this story.

Mama Jane, my great-grandmother, told the story as if unveiling a great, wonderful secret. My siblings and I believed that certain Africans shared this gift of taking to the air — "way up and over everything."